M U M U

and

KASSYAN OF FAIR SPRINGS

by

IVAN TURGENEV

Fredonia Books
Amsterdam, The Netherlands

Mumu and Kassyan of Fair Springs

by
Ivan Turgenev

ISBN: 1-4101-0289-0

Fredonia Books
Amsterdam, The Netherlands
http://www.fredoniabooks.com

KASSYAN OF FAIR SPRINGS

KASSYAN OF FAIR SPRINGS

I was returning from hunting in a jolting little trap, and overcome by the stifling heat of a cloudy summer day (it is well known that the heat is often more insupportable on such days than in bright days, especially when there is no wind), I dozed and was shaken about, resigning myself with sullen fortitude to being persecuted by the fine white dust which was incessantly raised from the beaten road by the warped and creaking wheels, when suddenly my attention was aroused by the extraordinary uneasiness and agitated movements of my coachman, who had till that instant been more soundly dozing than I. He began tugging at the reins, moved uneasily on the box, and started shouting to the horses, staring all the while in one direction. I looked round. We were driving through a wide ploughed plain; low hills, also ploughed over, ran in gently sloping, swelling waves over it; the eye took in some five miles of deserted country; in the distance

the round-scolloped tree-tops of some small
birch copses were the only objects to break
the almost straight line of the horizon. Narrow paths ran over the fields, disappeared
into the hollows, and wound round the hillocks.
On one of these paths, which happened to
run into our road five hundred paces ahead
of us, I made out a kind of procession. At
this my coachman was looking.

It was a funeral. In front, in a little cart
harnessed with one horse, and advancing at a
walking pace, came the priest; beside him
sat the deacon driving; behind the cart four
peasants, bareheaded, carried the coffin, covered with a white cloth; two women followed
the coffin. The shrill wailing voice of one of
them suddenly reached my ears; I listened;
she was intoning a dirge. Very dismal sounded this chanted, monotonous, hopelessly-sor-
rowful lament among the empty fields. The
coachman whipped up the horses; he wanted
to get in front of this procession. To meet
a corpse on the road is a bad omen. And he
did succeed in galloping ahead beyond this
path before the funeral had had time to turn
out of it into the high-road; but we had
hardly got a hundred paces beyond this point,
when suddenly our trap jolted violently,

heeled on one side, and all but overturned. The coachman pulled up the galloping horses, and spat with a gesture of his hand.

"What is it?" I asked.

My coachman got down without speaking or hurrying himself.

"But what is it?"

"The axle is broken . . . it caught fire," he replied gloomily, and he suddenly arranged the collar on the off-side horse with such indignation that it was almost pushed over, but it stood its ground, snorted, shook itself, and tranquilly began to scratch its foreleg below the knee with its teeth.

I got out and stood for some time on the road, a prey to a vague and unpleasant feeling of helplessness. The right wheel was almost completely bent in under the trap, and it seemed to turn its centre-piece upwards in dumb despair.

"What are we to do now?" I said at last.

"That's what's the cause of it!" said my coachman, pointing with his whip to the funeral procession, which had just turned into the highroad and was approaching us. "I have always noticed that," he went on; "it's a true saying—'Meet a corpse'—yes, indeed."

And again he began worrying the off-side horse, who, seeing his ill-humour, resolved to remain perfectly quiet, and contented itself with discreetly switching its tail now and then. I walked up and down a little while, and then stopped again before the wheel.

Meanwhile the funeral had come up to us. Quietly turning off the road on to the grass, the mournful procession moved slowly past us. My coachman and I took off our caps, saluted the priest, and exchanged glances with the bearers. They moved with difficulty under their burden, their broad chests standing out under the strain. Of the two women who followed the coffin, one was very old and pale; her set face, terribly distorted as it was by grief, still kept an expression of grave and severe dignity. She walked in silence, from time to time lifting her wasted hand to her thin drawn lips. The other, a young woman of five-and-twenty, had her eyes red and moist and her whole face swollen with weeping; as she passed us she ceased wailing, and hid her face in her sleeve. . . . But when the funeral had got round us and turned again into the road, her piteous, heart-piercing lament began again. My coachman followed the measured swaying of the coffin with his eyes in silence. Then he turned to me.

"It's Martin, the carpenter, they're burying," he said; "Martin of Ryaby."

"How do you know?"

"I know by the women. The old one is his mother, and the young one's his wife."

"Has he been ill, then?"

"Yes . . . fever. The day before yesterday the overseer sent for the doctor, but they did not find the doctor at home. He was a good carpenter; he drank a bit, but he was a good carpenter. See how upset his good woman is. . . . But, there; women's tears don't cost much, we know. Women's tears are only water . . . yes, indeed."

And he bent down, crept under the side-horse's trace, and seized the wooden yoke that passes over the horses' heads with both hands.

"Any way," I observed, "what are we going to do?"

My coachman just supported himself with his knees on the shaft-horse's shoulder, twice gave the back-strap a shake, and straightened the pad; then he crept out of the side-horse's trace again, and giving it a blow on the nose as he passed, went up to the wheel. He went

up to it, and, never taking his eyes off it,
slowly took out of the skirts of his coat a
box, slowly pulled open its lid by a strap,
slowly thrust into it his two fat fingers (which
pretty well filled it up), rolled and rolled
up some snuff, and creasing up his nose in
anticipation, helped himself to it several times
in succession, accompanying the snuff-taking
every time by a prolonged sneezing. Then, his
streaming eyes blinking faintly, he relapsed
into profound meditation.

"Well?" I said at last.

My coachman thrust his box carefully into
his pocket, brought his hat forward on to his
brows without the aid of his hand by a movement of his head, and gloomily got up on the
box.

"What are you doing?" I asked him, somewhat bewildered.

"Pray be seated," he replied calmly, pick-
ing up the reins.

"But how can we go on?"

"We will go on now."

"But the axle."

"Pray be seated."

"But the axle is broken."

"It is broken; but we will get to the settlement . . . at a walking pace, of course.

Over here, beyond the copse, on the right, is a settlement; they call it Yudino."

"And do you think we can get there?"

My coachman did not vouchsafe me a reply.

"I had better walk," I said.

"As you like . . . "   And he flourished his whip.   The horses started.

We did succeed in getting to the settlement, though the right front wheel was almost off, and turned in a very strange way.   On one hillock it almost flew off, but my coachman shouted in a voice of exasperation, and we descended it in safety.

Yudino settlement consisted of six little low-pitched huts, the walls of which had already begun to warp out of the perpendicular, though they had certainly not been long built; the back-yards of some of the huts were not even fenced in with a hedge.   As we drove into this settlement we did not meet a single living soul; there were no hens even to be seen in the street, and no dogs, but one black crop-tailed cur, which at our approach leaped hurriedly out of a perfectly dry and empty trough, to which it must have been driven by thirst, and at once, without barking, rushed headlong under a gate.   I went up to the first hut, opened the door into the outer

room, and called for the master of the house.
No one answered me. I called once more; the
hungry mewing of a cat sounded behind the
other door. I pushed it open with my foot;
a thin cat ran up and down near me, her
green eyes glittering in the dark. I put my
head into the room and looked round; it was
empty, dark, and smoky. I returned to the
yard, and there was no one there either. . . .
A calf lowed behind the paling; a lame grey
goose waddled a little away. I passed on to
the second hut. Not a soul in the second hut
either. I went into the yard. . . .

In the very middle of the yard, in the glaring sunlight, there lay, with his face on the
ground and a cloak thrown over his head,
a boy, as it seemed to me. In a thatched
shed a few paces from him a thin little nag
with broken harness was standing near a
wretched little cart. The sunshine falling in
streaks through the narrow cracks in the
dilapidated roof, striped his shaggy, reddish-
brown coat in small bands of light. Above,
in the high bird-house, starlings were chat-
tering and looking down inquisitively from
their airy home. I went up to the sleeping
figure and began to awaken him.

He lifted his head, saw me, and at once

jumped up on to his feet. . . . "What? what do you want? what is it?" he muttered, half asleep.

I did not answer him at once; I was so much impressed by his appearance.

Picture to yourself a little creature of fifty years old, with a little round wrinkled face, a sharp nose, little, scarcely visible, brown eyes, and thick curly black hair, which stood out on his tiny head like the cap on the top of a mushroom. His whole person was excessively thin and weakly, and it is absolutely impossible to translate into words the extraordinary strangeness of his expression.

"What do you want?" he asked me again. I explained to him what was the matter; he listened, slowly blinking, without taking his eyes off me.

"So cannot we get a new axle?" I said finally; "I will gladly pay for it."

"But who are you? Hunters, eh?" he asked, scanning me from head to foot.

"Hunters."

"You shoot the fowls of heaven, I suppose? . . . the wild things of the woods? . . . And is it not a sin to kill God's birds, to shed the innocent blood?"

The strange old man spoke in a very drawling tone. The sound of his voice also astonished me. There was none of the weakness of age to be heard in it; it was marvellously sweet, young and almost feminine in its softness.

"I have no axle," he added after a brief silence. "That thing will not suit you." He pointed to his cart. "You have, I expect, a large trap."

"But can I get one in the village?"

"Not much of a village here! . . . No one has an axle here. . . . And there is no one at home either; they are all at work. You must go on," he announced suddenly; and he lay down again on the ground.

I had not at all expected this conclusion.

"Listen, old man," I said, touching him on the shoulder; "do me a kindness, help me."

"Go on, in God's name! I am tired; I have driven into the town," he said, and drew his cloak over his head.

"But pray do me a kindness," I said. "I . . . I will pay for it."

"I don't want your money."

"But please, old man."

He half raised himself and sat up, crossing his little legs.

"I could take you perhaps to the clearing.

Some merchants have bought the forest here
—God be their judge! They are cutting
down the forest, and they have built a counting-house there—God be their judge! You
might order an axle of them there, or buy
one ready made."

"Splendid!" I cried delighted; "splendid!
let us go."

"An oak axle, a good one," he continued,
not getting up from his place.

"And is it far to this clearing?"

"Three miles."

"Come, then! we can drive there in your
trap."

"Oh, no. . . ."

"Come, let us go," I said; "let us go, old
man! The coachman is waiting for us in
the road."

The old man rose unwillingly and followed
me into the street. We found my coachman
in an irritable frame of mind; he had tried
to water his horses, but the water in the well,
it appeared, was scanty in quantity and bad
in taste, and water is the first consideration
with coachmen. . . . However, he grinned
at the sight of the old man, nodded his head
and cried: "Hallo! Kassyanushka! good
health to you!"

"Good health to you, Erofay, upright man!"
replied Kassyan in a dejected voice.

I at once made known his suggestion to
the coachman; Erofay expressed his approval
of it and drove into the yard.   While he was
busy deliberately unharnessing the horses, the
old man stood leaning with his shoulders
against the gate, and looking disconsolately
first at him and then at me.   He seemed in some
uncertainty of mind; he was not very pleased,
as it seemed to me, at our sudden visit.

"So they have transported you too?" Erofay
asked him suddenly, lifting the wooden arch
of the harness.

"Yes."

"Ugh!" said my coachman between his
teeth.   "You know Martin the carpenter.
. . . Of course, you know Martin of Ryaby?"

"Yes."

"Well, he is dead.   We have just met his
coffin." Kassyan shuddered.

"Dead?" he said, and his head sank de-
jectedly.

"Yes, he is dead.   Why didn't you cure
him, eh?   You know they say you cure folks;
you're a doctor."

My coachman was apparently laughing and
jeering at the old man.

"And is this your trap, pray?" he added, with a shrug of his shoulders in its direction.

"Yes."

"Well, a trap . . . a fine trap!" he repeated, and taking it by the shafts almost turned it completely upside down. "A trap! . . . But what will you drive in it to the clearing? . . . You can't harness our horses in these shafts; our horses are all too big."

"I don't know," replied Kassyan, "what you are going to drive; that beast perhaps," he added with a sigh.

"That?" broke in Erofay, and going up to Kassyan's nag, he tapped it disparagingly on the back with the third finger of his right hand. "See," he added contemptuously, "it's asleep, the scarecrow!"

I asked Erofay to harness it as quickly as he could. I wanted to drive myself with Kassyan to the clearing; grouse are fond of such places. When the little cart was quite ready, and I, together with my dog, had been installed in the warped wicker body of it, and Kassyan huddled up into a little ball, with still the same dejected expression on his face, had taken his seat in front, Erofay came up to me and whispered with an air of mystery:

"You did well, your honour, to drive with

him. He is such a queer fellow; he's cracked,
you know, and his nickname is the Flea.
I don't know how you managed to make him
out. . . ."

I tried to say to Erofay that so far Kassyan had seemed to me a very sensible man;
but my coachman continued at once in the
same voice:

"But you keep a look-out where he is driving you to. And, your honour, be pleased to
choose the axle yourself; be pleased to choose
a sound one. . . . Well, Flea," he added
aloud, "could I get a bit of bread in your
house?"

"Look about; you may find some," answered
Kassyan. He pulled the reins and we rolled
away.

His little horse, to my genuine astonishment, did not go badly. Kassyan preserved
an obstinate silence the whole way, and made
abrupt and unwilling answers to my questions.
We quickly reached the clearing, and then
made our way to the counting-house, a lofty
cottage, standing by itself over a small gully,
which had been dammed up and converted
into a pool. In this counting-house I found
two young merchants' clerks, with snow-white
teeth, sweet and soft eyes, sweet and subtle

words, and sweet and wily smiles. I bought an axle of them and returned to the clearing. I thought that Kassyan would stay with the horse and await my return; but he suddenly came up to me.

"Are you going to shoot birds, eh?" he said.

"Yes, if I come across any."

"I will come with you. . . . Can I?"

"Certainly, certainly."

So we went together. The land cleared was about a mile in length. I must confess I watched Kassyan more than my dogs. He had been aptly called "Flea." His little black uncovered head (though his hair, indeed, was as good a covering as any cap) seemed to flash hither and thither among the bushes. He walked extraordinarily swiftly, and seemed always hopping up and down as he moved; he was for ever stooping down to pick herbs of some kind, thrusting them into his bosom, muttering to himself, and constantly looking at me and my dog with such a strange searching gaze. Among low bushes and in clearings there are often little grey birds which constantly flit from tree to tree, and which whistle as they dart away. Kassyan mimicked them, answered their calls; a

young quail flew from between his feet, chir-
ruping, and he chirruped in imitation of him;
a lark began to fly down above him, moving
his wings and singing melodiously: Kassyan
joined in his song.   He did not speak to me
at all. . . .

The weather was glorious, even more so
than before; but the heat was no less.   Over
the clear sky the high thin clouds were hardly
stirred, yellowish-white, like snow lying late
in spring, flat and drawn out like rolled-up
sails.   Slowly but perceptibly their fringed
edges, soft and fluffy as cotton-wool, changed
at every moment; they were melting away,
even these clouds, and no shadow fell from
them.   I strolled about the clearing for a
long while with Kassyan.   Young shoots,
which had not yet had time to grow more
than a yard high, surrounded the low blackened stumps with their smooth slender stems;
and spongy funguses with grey edges—the
same of which they make tinder—clung to
these; strawberry plants flung their rosy ten-
drils over them; mushrooms squatted close in
groups.   The feet were constantly caught and
entangled in the long grass, that was parched
in the scorching sun; the eyes were dazzled
on all sides by the glaring metallic glitter

on the young reddish leaves of the trees; on all sides were the variegated blue clusters of vetch, the golden cups of bloodwort, and the half-lilac, half-yellow blossoms of the heart's-ease. In some places near the disused paths, on which the tracks of wheels were marked by streaks on the fine bright grass, rose piles of wood, blackened by wind and rain, laid in yard-lengths; there was a faint shadow cast from them in slanting oblongs; there was no other shade anywhere. A light breeze rose, then sank again; suddenly it would blow straight in the face and seem to be rising; everything would begin to rustle merrily, to nod, to shake around one; the supple tops of the ferns bow down gracefully, and one rejoices in it, but at once it dies away again, and all is at rest once more. Only the grasshoppers chirrup in chorus with frenzied energy, and wearisome is this unceasing, sharp dry sound. It is in keeping with the persistent heat of mid-day; it seems akin to it, as though evoked by it out of the glowing earth.

Without having started one single covey we at last reached another clearing. There the aspentrees had only lately been felled, and lay stretched mournfully on the ground, crushing the grass and small undergrowth below them: on some the leaves were still green, though they were already dead, and hung limply from the motionless branches; on others they were crumpled and dried up. Fresh golden-white chips lay in heaps round the stumps that were covered with bright drops; a peculiar, very pleasant, pungent odour rose from them. Farther away, nearer the wood, sounded the dull blows of the axe, and from time to time, bowing and spreading wide its arms, a bushy tree fell slowly and majestically to the ground.

For a long time I did not come upon a single bird; at last a corncrake flew out of a thick clump of young oak across the wormwood springing up round it. I fired; it turned over in the air and fell. At the sound of the shot, Kassyan quickly covered his eyes with his hand, and he did not stir till I had reloaded the gun and picked up the bird. When I had moved farther on, he went up to the place where the wounded bird had fallen, bent down to the grass, on which some drops of blood were sprinkled, shook his head, and looked in dismay at me. . . . I heard him afterwards whispering: "A sin! . . . Ah, yes, it's a sin!"

The heat forced us at last to go into the wood. I flung myself down under a high nut-bush, over which a slender young maple gracefully stretched its light branches. Kassyan sat down on the thick trunk of a felled birch-tree. I looked at him. The leaves faintly stirred overhead, and their thin greenish shadows crept softly to and fro over his feeble body, muffled in a dark coat, and over his little face. He did not lift his head. Bored by his silence, I lay on my back and began to admire the tranquil play of the tangled foliage on the background of the bright, far away sky. A marvellously sweet occupation it is to lie on one's back in a wood and gaze upwards! You may fancy you are looking into a bottomless sea; that it stretches wide below you; that the trees are not rising out of the earth, but, like the roots of gigantic weeds, are dropping—falling straight down into those glassy, limpid depths; the leaves on the trees are at one moment transparent as emeralds, the next, they condense into golden, almost black green. Somewhere, afar off, at the end of a slender twig, a single leaf hangs motionless against the blue patch of transparent sky, and beside it another trembles with the motion of a fish on the line, as though moving of its own will, not shaken by the wind. Round white clouds float calmly across, and calmly pass away like submarine islands; and suddenly, all this ocean, this shining ether, these branches and leaves steeped in sunlight—all is rippling, quivering in fleeting brilliance, and a fresh trembling whisper awakens like the tiny, incessant plash of suddenly stirred eddies. One does not move—one looks, and no word can tell what peace, what joy, what sweetness reigns in the heart. One looks: the deep, pure blue stirs on one's lips a smile, innocent as itself; like the clouds over the sky, and, as it were, with them, happy memories pass in slow procession over the soul, and still one fancies one's gaze goes deeper and deeper, and draws one with it up into that peaceful, shining immensity, and that one cannot be brought back from that height, that depth. . . .

"Master, master!" cried Kassyan suddenly in his musical voice.

I raised myself in surprise: up till then he had scarcely replied to my questions, and now he suddenly addressed me of himself.

"What is it?" I asked.

"What did you kill the bird for?" he began, looking me straight in the face.

"What for? Corncrake is game; one can eat it."

"That was not what you killed it for, master, as though you were going to eat it! You killed it for amusement."

"Well, you yourself, I suppose, ate geese or chickens?"

"Those birds are provided by God for man, but the corncrake is a wild bird of the woods: and not he alone; many they are, the wild things of the woods and the fields, and the wild things of the rivers and marshes and moors, flying on high or creeping below; and a sin it is to slay them: let them live their allotted life upon the earth. But for man another food has been provided; his food is other, and other his sustenance: bread, the good gift of God, and the water of heaven, and the tame beasts that have come down to us from our fathers of old."

I looked in astonishment at Kassyan. His words flowed freely; he did not hesitate for a word; he spoke with quiet inspiration and gentle dignity, sometimes closing his eyes.

"So is it sinful, then, to kill fish, according to you?" I asked.

"Fishes have cold blood," he replied with conviction. "The fish is a dumb creature; it knows neither fear nor rejoicing. The fish is a voiceless creature. The fish does not feel; the blood in it is not living. . . . Blood," he continued, after a pause, "blood is a holy thing! God's sun does not look upon blood; it is hidden away from the light . . . it is a great sin to bring blood into the light of day; a great sin and horror. . . . Ah, a great sin!"

He sighed, and his head drooped forward. I looked, I confess, in absolute amazement at the strange old man. His language did not sound like the language of a peasant; the common people do not speak like that, nor those who aim at fine speaking. His speech was meditative, grave, and curious. . . . I had never heard anything like it.

"Tell me, please, Kassyan," I began, without taking my eyes off his slightly flushed face, "what is your occupation?"

He did not answer my question at once. His eyes strayed uneasily for an instant.

"I live as the Lord commands," he brought out at last; "and as for occupation—no, I have no occupation. I've never been very clever from a child: I work when I can: I'm

not much of a workman—how should I be?
I have no health; my hands are awkward. In
the spring I catch nightingales."

"You catch nightingales? . . . But didn't
you tell me that we must not touch any of
the wild things of the woods and the fields,
and so on?"

"We must not kill them, of a certainty;
death will take its own without that. Look
at Martin the carpenter; Martin lived, and
his wife was not long, but he died; his wife
now grieves for her husband, for her little
children. . . . Neither for man nor beast is
there any charm against death. Death does
not hasten, nor is there any escaping it; but
we must not aid death. . . . And I do not
kill nightingales—God forbid! I do not catch
them to harm them, to spoil their lives, but
for the pleasure of men, for their comfort
and delight."

"Do you go to Kursk to catch them?"

"Yes, I go to Kursk, and farther too, at
times. I pass nights in the marshes, or at
the edge of the forests; I am alone at night
in the fields, in the thickets; there the curlews
call and the hares squeak and the wild ducks
lift up their voices. . . . I note them at evening; at morning I give ear to them; at day-

break I cast my net over the bushes. . . .
There are nightingales that sing so pitifully
sweet . . . yea, pitifully."

"And do you sell them?"

"I give them to good people."

"And what are you doing now?"

"What am I doing?"

"Yes, how are you employed?"

The old man was silent for a little.

"I am not employed at all. . . . I am a
poor workman. But I can read and write."

"You can read?"

"Yes, I can read and write. I learnt, by
the help of God and good people."

"Have you a family?"

"No, not a family."

"How so? . . . Are they dead, then?"

"No, but . . . I have never been lucky in
life. But all that is in God's hands; we are
all in God's hands; and a man should be
righteous—that is all! Upright before God,
that is it."

"And you have no kindred?"

"Yes . . . well. . . ."

The old man was confused.

"Tell me, please," I began: "I heard my
coachman ask you why you did not cure
Martin? You cure disease?"

"Your coachman is a righteous man," Kassyan answered thoughtfully. "I too am not
without sin. They call me a doctor. . . . Me
a doctor, indeed! And who can heal the sick?
That is all a gift from God. But there are
. . . yes, there are herbs, and there are flow-
ers; they are of use, of a certainty. There is
plantain, for instance, a herb good for man;
there is bud-marigold too; it is not sinful to
speak of them: they are holy herbs of God.
Then there are others not so; and they may
be of use, but it's a sin; and to speak of them
is a sin. Still, with prayer, may be. . . .
And doubtless there are such words. . . .
But who has faith, shall be saved," he added,
dropping his voice.

"You did not give Martin anything?" I
asked.

"I heard of it too late," replied the old
man. "But what of it! Each man's destiny
is written from his birth. The carpenter
Martin was not to live; he was not to live
upon the earth: that was what it was. No,
when a man is not to live on the earth, him
the sunshine does not warm like another, and
him the bread does not nourish and make
strong; it is as though something is drawing
him away. . . . Yes: God rest his soul!"

"Have you been settled long amongst us?"
I asked him after a short pause.

Kassyan started.

"No, not long; four years. In the old
master's time we always lived in our old
houses, but the trustees transported us. Our
old master was a kind heart, a man of peace
—the Kingdom of Heaven be his! The trustees doubtless judged righteously."

"And where did you live before?"

"At Fair Springs."

"Is it far from here?"

"A hundred miles."

"Well, were you better off there?"

"Yes . . . yes, there there was open country, with rivers; it was our home: here we
are cramped and parched up. . . . Here we
are strangers. There at home, at Fair
Springs, you could get up on to a hill—and
ah, my God, what a sight you could see!
Streams and plains and forests, and there was
a church, and then came plains beyond. You
could see far, very far. Yes, how far you
could look—you could look and look, ah,
yes! Here, doubtless, the soil is better; it is
clay—good fat clay, as the peasants say;
for me the corn grows well enough every-
where."

"Confess then, old man; you would like to visit your birth-place again?"

"Yes, I should like to see it. Still, all places are good. I am a man without kin, without neighbours. And, after all, do you gain much, pray, by staying at home? But, behold! as you walk, and as you walk," he went on, raising his voice, "the heart grows lighter, of a truth. And the sun shines upon you, and you are in the sight of God, and the singing comes more tunefully. Here, you look—what herb is growing; you look on it— you pick it. Here water runs, perhaps— spring water, a source of pure holy water; so you drink of it—you look on it too. The birds of heaven sing. . . . And beyond Kursk come the steppes, that steppes-country: ah, what a marvel, what a delight for man! what freedom, what a blessing of God! And they go on, folks tell, even to the warm seas where dwells the sweet-voiced bird, the Hamayune, and from the trees the leaves fall not, neither in autumn nor in winter, and apples grow of gold, on silver branches, and every man lives in uprightness and content. And I would go even there. . . . Have I journeyed so little already! I have been to Romyon and to Simbirsk the fair city, and even to Moscow

of the golden domes; I have been to Oka
the good nurse, and to Tsna the dove, and to
our mother Volga, and many folks, good
Christians have I seen, and noble cities I
have visited. . . . Well, I would go thither
. . . yes . . . and more too . . . and I am
not the only one, I a poor sinner . . . many
other Christians go in bast-shoes, roaming
over the world, seeking truth, yea! . . . For
what is there at home? No righteousness in
man—it's that."

These last words Kassyan uttered quickly,
almost unintelligibly; then he said something
more which I could not catch at all, and such
a strange expression passed over his face that
I involuntarily recalled the epithet "cracked."
He looked down, cleared his throat, and
seemed to come to himself again.

"What sunshine!" he murmured in a low
voice. "It is a blessing, oh, Lord! What
warmth in the woods!"

He gave a movement of the shoulders and
fell into silence. With a vague look round
him he began softly to sing. I could not catch
all the words of his slow chant; I heard the
following:

> "They call me Kassyan,
> But my nickname's the Flea."

"Oh!" I thought, "so he improvises." Suddenly he started and ceased singing, looking intently at a thick part of the wood. I turned and saw a little peasant girl, about seven years old, in a blue frock, with a checked handkerchief over her head, and a woven bark-basket in her little bare sunburnt hand. She had certainly not expected to meet us; she had, as they say, "stumbled upon" us, and she stood motionless in a shady recess among the thick foliage of the nut-trees, looking dismayed at me with her black eyes. I had scarcely time to catch a glimpse of her; she dived behind a tree.

"Annushka! Annushka! come here, don't be afraid!" cried the old man caressingly.

"I'm afraid," came her shrill voice.

"Don't be afraid, don't be afraid; come to me."

Annushka left her hiding place in silence, walked softly round—her little childish feet scarcely sounded on the thick grass—and came out of the bushes near the old man. She was not a child of seven, as I had fancied at first, from her diminutive stature, but a girl of thirteen or fourteen. Her whole person was small and thin, but very neat and graceful, and her pretty little face was strikingly like Kassyan's own, though he was certainly not handsome. There were the same thin features, and the same strange expression, shy and confiding, melancholy and shrewd, and her gestures were the same. . . . Kassyan kept his eyes fixed on her; she took her stand at his side.

"Well, have you picked any mushrooms?" he asked.

"Yes," she answered with a shy smile.

"Did you find many?"

"Yes." (She stole a swift look at him and smiled again.)

"Are they white ones?"

"Yes."

"Show me, show me. . . . (She slipped the basket off her arm and half-lifted the big burdock leaf which covered up the mushrooms.) "Ah!" said Kassyan, bending down over the basket; "what splendid ones! Well done, Annushka!"

"She's your daughter, Kassyan, isn't she?" I asked. (Annushka's face flushed faintly.)

"No, well, a relative," replied Kassyan with affected indifference. "Come, Annushka, run along," he added at once, "run along, and God be with you! And take care."

"But why should she go on foot?" I interrupted. "We could take her with us."

Annushka blushed like a poppy, grasped the handle of her basket with both hands, and looked in trepidation at the old man.

"No, she will get there all right," he answered in the same languid and indifferent voice. "Why not? . . . She will get there. . . . Run along."

Annushka went rapidly away into the forest. Kassyan looked after her, then looked down and smiled to himself. In this prolonged smile, in the few words he had spoken to Annushka, and in the very sound of his voice when he spoke to her, there was an intense, indescribable love and tenderness. He looked again in the direction she had gone, again smiled to himself, and, passing his hand across his face, he nodded his head several times.

"Why did you send her away so soon?" I asked him. "I would have bought her mushrooms."

"Well, you can buy them there at home just the same, sir, if you like," he answered, for the first time using the formal "sir" in addressing me.

"She's very pretty, your girl."

"No . . . only so-so," he answered, with seeming reluctance, and from that instant he relapsed into the same uncommunicative mood as at first.

Seeing that all my efforts to make him talk again were fruitless, I went off into the clearing. Meantime the heat had somewhat abated; but my ill-success, or, as they say among us, my "ill-luck," continued, and I returned to the settlement with nothing but one corncrake and the new axle. Just as we were driving into the yard, Kassyan suddenly turned to me.

"Master, master," he began, "do you know I have done you a wrong; it was I cast a spell to keep all the game off."

"How so?"

"Oh, I can do that. Here you have a well-trained dog and a good one, but he could do nothing. When you think of it, what are men? what are they? Here's a beast; what have they made of him?"

It would have been useless for me to try to convince Kassyan of the impossibility of "casting a spell" on game, and so I made him no reply. Meantime we had turned into the yard.

Annushka was not in the hut: she had had

time to get there before us, and to leave her basket of mushrooms.   Erofay fitted in the new axle, first exposing it to a severe and most unjust criticism; and an hour later I set off, leaving a small sum of money with Kassyan, which at first he was unwilling to accept, but afterwards, after a moment's thought, holding it in his hand, he put it in his bosom.   In the course of this hour he had scarcely uttered a single word; he stood as before, leaning against the gate.   He made no reply to the reproaches of my coachman, and took leave very coldly of me.

Directly I turned round, I could see that my worthy Erofay was in a gloomy frame of mind. . . . To be sure, he had found nothing to eat in the country; the only water for his horses was bad.   We drove off.   With dissatisfaction expressed even in the back of his head, he sat on the box, burning to begin to talk to me.   While waiting for me to begin by some question, he confined himself to a low muttering in an undertone, and some rather caustic instructions to the horses.   "A village," he muttered; "call that a village? You ask for a drop of kvas—not a drop of kvas even. . . . Ah, Lord! . . . And the water—simply filth!"   (He spat loudly.)

"Not a cucumber, nor kvas, nor nothing. . . .
Now, then!" he added aloud, turning to the
right trace-horse; "I know you, you humbug."
(And he gave him a cut with the whip.)
"That horse has learnt to shirk his work en-
tirely, and yet he was a willing beast once.
Now, then—look alive!"

"Tell me, please, Erofay," I began, "what
sort of a man is Kassyan?"

Erofay did not answer me at once: he was,
in general, a reflective and deliberate fellow;
but I could see directly that my question was
soothing and cheering to him.

"The Flea?" he said at last, gathering up
the reins; "he's a queer fellow; yes, a crazy
chap; such a queer fellow, you wouldn't find
another like him in a hurry. You know, for
example, he's for all the world like our roan
horse here; he gets out of everything—out
of work, that's to say. But, then, what sort
of workman could he be? . . . He's hardly
body enough to keep his soul in . . . but
still, of course. . . . He's been like that
from a child up, you know. At first he followed his uncle's business as a carrier—there
were three of them in the business; but then
he got tired of it, you know—he threw it up.
He began to live at home, but he could not

keep at home long; he's so restless—a regular
flea, in fact. He happened, by good luck,
to have a good master—he didn't worry him.
Well, so ever since he has been wandering
about like a lost sheep. And then, he's so
strange; there no understanding him. Sometimes he'll be as silent as a post, and then
he'll begin talking, and God knows what he'll
say! Is that good manners, pray? He's an
absurd fellow, that he is. But he sings well,
for all that."

"And does he cure people, really?"

"Cure people! . . . Well, how should he?
A fine sort of doctor! Though he did cure
me of the king's evil, I must own. . . . But
how can he? He's a stupid fellow, that's
what he is," he added, after a moment's
pause.

"Have you known him long?"

"A long while. I was his neighbour at
Sitchovka up at Fair Springs."

"And what of that girl—who met us in the
wood, Annushka—what relation is she to
him?"

Erofay looked at me over his shoulder, and
grinned all over his face.

"He, he! . . . yes, they are relations. She
is an orphan; she has no mother, and it's not

even known who her mother was. But she
must be a relation; she's too much like him.
. . . Anyway, she lives with him. She's a
smart girl, there's no denying; a good girl;
and as for the old man, she's simply the apple
of his eye; she's a good girl. And, do you
know, you wouldn't believe it, but do you
know, he's managed to teach Annushka to
read? Well, well! that's quite like him; he's
such an extraordinary fellow, such a change-
able fellow; there's no reckoning on him,
really. . . . Eh! eh! eh!" My coachman
suddenly interrupted himself, and stopping
the horses, he bent over on one side and began sniffing. "Isn't there a smell of burning? Yes! Why, that new axle, I do de-
clare! . . . I thought I'd greased it. . . .
We must get on to some water; why, here is
a puddle, just right."

And Erofay slowly got off his seat, untied
the pail, went to the pool, and coming back,
listened with a certain satisfaction to the hiss-
ing of the box of the wheel as the water suddenly touched it. . . . Six times during some
eight miles he had to pour water on the
smouldering axle, and it was quite evening
when we got home at last.

MUMU

MUMU

In one of the outlying streets of Moscow, in a grey house with white columns and a balcony, warped all askew, there was once living a lady, a widow, surrounded by a numerous household of serfs. Her sons were in the government service at Petersburg; her daughters were married; she went out very little, and in solitude lived through the last years of her miserly and dreary old age. Her day, a joyless and gloomy day, had long been over; but the evening of her life was blacker than night.

Of all her servants, the most remarkable personage was the porter, Gerasim, a man full twelve inches over the normal height, of heroic build, and deaf and dumb from his birth. The lady, his owner, had brought him up from the village where he lived alone in a little hut, apart from his brothers, and was reckoned about the most punctual of her peasants in the payment of the seignorial dues. Endowed with extraordinary strength, he did the work of four men; work flew apace under his hands, and it was a pleasant sight to see him when he was ploughing, while, with his huge palms pressing hard upon the plough, he seemed alone, unaided by his poor horse, to cleave the yielding bosom of the earth, or when, about St. Peter's Day, he plied his scythe with a furious energy that might have mown a young birch copse up by the roots, or swiftly and untiringly wielded a flail over two yards long; while the hard oblong muscles of his shoulders rose and fell like a lever. His perpetual silence lent a solemn dignity to his unwearying labour. He was a splendid peasant, and, except for his affliction, any girl would have been glad to marry him. . . . But now they had taken Gerasim to Moscow, bought him boots, had him made a full-skirted coat for summer, a sheepskin for winter, put into his hand a broom and a spade, and appointed him porter.

At first he intensely disliked his new mode of life. From his childhood he had been used to field labour, to village life. Shut off by his affliction from the society of men, he had grown up, dumb and mighty, as a tree grows on a fruitful soil. When he was transported to the town, he could not understand what was being done with him; he was miserable and stupefied, with the stupefaction of some strong young bull, taken straight from the meadow, where the rich grass stood up to his belly, taken and put in the truck of a railway train, and there, while smoke and sparks and gusts of steam puff out upon the sturdy beast, he is whirled onwards, whirled along with loud roar and whistle, whither—God knows! What Gerasim had to do in his new duties seemed a mere trifle to him after his hard toil as a peasant; in half-an-hour, all his work was done, and he would once more stand stock-still in the middle of the courtyard, staring open-mouthed at all the passers-by, as though trying to wrest from them the explanation of his perplexing position; or he would suddenly go off into some corner, and flinging a long way off the broom or the spade, throw himself on his face on the ground, and lie for hours together without stirring, like a caged beast. But man gets used to anything, and Gerasim got used at last to living in town. He had little work to do; his whole duty consisted in keeping the courtyard clean, bringing in a barrel of water twice a day, splitting and dragging in wood for the kitchen and the house, keeping out strangers, and watching at night. And it must be said he did his duty zealously. In his courtyard there was never a shaving lying about, never a speck of dust; if sometimes, in the muddy season, the wretched nag, put under his charge for fetching water, got stuck in the road, he would simply give it a shove with his shoulder, and set not only the cart but the horse itself moving. If he set to chopping wood, the axe fairly rang like glass, and chips and chunks flew in all directions. And as for strangers, after he had one night caught two thieves and knocked their heads together— knocked them so that there was not the slightest need to take them to the police-station afterwards—every one in the neighbourhood began to feel a great respect for him; even those who came in the day-time, by no means robbers, but simply unknown persons, at the sight of the terrible porter, waved and shouted to him as though he could hear their shouts. With all the rest of the servants, Gerasim was on terms, hardly friendly—they were afraid of him—but familiar; he regarded them as his fellows. They explained themselves to him by signs, and he

understood them, and exactly carried out all
orders, but knew his own rights too, and
soon no one dared to take his seat at the
table. Gerasim was altogether of a strict
and serious temper, he liked order in everything; even the cocks did not dare to fight
in his presence, or woe betide them! directly
he caught sight of them, he would seize them
by the legs, swing them ten times round in
the air like a wheel, and throw them in dif-
ferent directions. There were geese, too,
kept in the yard; but the goose, as is well
known, is a dignified and reasonable bird;
Gerasim felt a respect for them, looked after
them, and fed them; he was himself not un-
like a gander of the steppes. He was as-
signed a little garret over the kitchen; he
arranged it himself to his own liking, made
a bedstead in it of oak boards on four stumps
of wood for legs—a truly Titanic bedstead;
one might have put a ton or two on it—it
would not have bent under the load; under
the bed was a solid chest; in a corner stood a
little table of the same strong kind, and near
the table a three-legged stool, so solid and
squat that Gerasim himself would sometimes
pick it up and drop it again with a smile of
delight. The garret was locked up by means

of a padlock that looked like a kalatch or
basket-shaped loaf, only black; the key of
this padlock Gerasim always carried about
him in his girdle. He did not like people to
come to his garret.

So passed a year, at the end of which a
little incident befell Gerasim.

The old lady, in whose service he lived as
porter, adhered in everything to the ancient
ways, and kept a large number of servants.
In her house were not only laundresses,
sempstresses, carpenters, tailors and tailor-
esses, there was even a harness-maker—he
was reckoned as a veterinary surgeon, too,—
and a doctor for the servants; there was
a household doctor for the mistress; there was,
lastly, a shoemaker, by name Kapiton Klimov, a sad drunkard. Klimov regarded himself as an injured creature, whose merits
were unappreciated, a cultivated man from
Petersburg, who ought not to be living in
Moscow without occupation—in the wilds, so
to speak; and if he drank, as he himself
expressed it emphatically, with a blow on
his chest, it was sorrow drove him to it. So
one day his mistress had a conversation about
him with her head steward, Gavrila, a man
whom, judging solely from his little yellow

eyes and nose like a duck's beak, fate itself,
it seemed, had marked out as a person in
authority. The lady expressed her regret at
the corruption of the morals of Kapiton, who
had, only the evening before, been picked up
somewhere in the street.

"Now, Gavrila," she observed, all of a
sudden, "now, if we were to marry him, what
do you think, perhaps he would be steadier?"

"Why not marry him, indeed, 'm? He
could be married, 'm," answered Gavrila,
"and it would be a very good thing, to be
sure, 'm."

"Yes; only who is to marry him?"

"Ay, 'm. But that's at your pleasure, 'm.
He may, any way, so to say, be wanted for
something; he can't be turned adrift altogether."

"I fancy he likes Tatiana."

Gavrila was on the point of making some
reply, but he shut his lips tightly.

"Yes! . . . let him marry Tatiana," the
lady decided, taking a pinch of snuff com-
placently. "Do you hear?"

"Yes, 'm," Gavrila articulated, and he
withdrew.

Returning to his own room (it was in a
little lodge, and was almost filled up with

metal-bound trunks), Gavrila first sent his
wife away, and then sat down at the window
and pondered. His mistress's unexpected ar-
rangement had clearly put him in a difficulty. At last he got up and sent to call
Kapiton. Kapiton made his appearance. . . .
But before reporting their conversation to
the reader, we consider it not out of place to
relate in few words who was this Tatiana,
whom it was to be Kapiton's lot to marry,
and why the great lady's order had disturbed
the steward.

Tatiana, one of the laundresses referred
to above (as a trained and skilful laundress
she was in charge of the fine linen only), was
a woman of twenty-eight, thin, fair-haired,
with moles on her left cheek. Moles on the
left cheek are regarded as of evil omen in
Russia—a token of unhappy life. . . . Tatiana could not boast of her good luck. From
her earliest youth she had been badly treated;
she had done the work of two, and had never
known affection; she had been poorly clothed
and had received the smallest wages. Relations she had practically none; an uncle she
had once had, a butler, left behind in the
country as useless, and other uncles of hers
were peasants—that was all. At one time

she had passed for a beauty, but her good
looks were very soon over. In disposition,
she was very meek, or, rather, scared; towards herself, she felt perfect indifference;
of others, she stood in mortal dread; she
thought of nothing but how to get her work
done in good time, never talked to any one,
and trembled at the very name of her mistress, though the latter scarcely knew her
by sight. When Gerasim was brought from
the country, she was ready to die with fear
on seeing his huge figure, tried all she could
to avoid meeting him, even dropped her eye-
lids when sometimes she chanced to run past
him, hurrying from the house to the laundry.
Gerasim at first paid no special attention to
her, then he used to smile when she came his
way, then he began even to stare admiringly
at her, and at last he never took his eyes
off her. She took his fancy, whether by the
mild expression of her face or the timidity
of her movements, who can tell? So one
day she was stealing across the yard, with
a starched dressing-jacket of her mistress's
carefully poised on her outspread fingers
. . . some one suddenly grasped her vigorously by the elbow; she turned round and
fairly screamed; behind her stood Gerasim.

With a foolish smile, making inarticulate caressing grunts, he held out to her a ginger-
bread cock with gold tinsel on his tail and
wings. She was about to refuse it, but he
thrust it forcibly into her hand, shook his
head, walked away, and turning round, once
more grunted something very affectionately
to her. From that day forward he gave her
no peace; wherever she went, he was on the
spot at once, coming to meet her, smiling,
grunting, waving his hands; all at once he
would pull a ribbon out of the bosom of his
smock and put it in her hand, or would
sweep the dust out of her way. The poor
girl simply did not know how to behave or
what to do. Soon the whole household knew
of the dumb porter's wiles; jeers, jokes, sly
hints were showered upon Tatiana. At Gerasim, however, it was not every one who
would dare to scoff; he did not like jokes;
indeed, in his presence, she, too, was left in
peace. Whether she liked it or not, the girl
found herself to be under his protection.
Like all deaf-mutes, he was very suspicious,
and very readily perceived when they were
laughing at him or at her. One day, at dinner, the wardrobe-keeper, Tatiana's superior,
fell to nagging, as it is called, at her, and

brought the poor thing to such a state that
she did not know where to look, and was almost crying with vexation. Gerasim got up
all of a sudden, stretched out his gigantic
hand, laid it on the wardrobe-maid's head,
and looked into her face with such grim
ferocity that her head positively flopped upon
the table. Every one was still. Gerasim
took up his spoon again and went on with
his cabbage-soup. "Look at him, the dumb
devil, the wood-demon!" they all muttered
in under-tones, while the wardrobe-maid got
up and went out into the maids' room. Another time, noticing that Kapiton—the same
Kapiton who was the subject of the conversation reported above—was gossiping somewhat too attentively with Tatiana, Gerasim
beckoned him to him, led him into the cart-
shed, and taking up a shaft that was standing in a corner by one end, lightly, but most
significantly, menaced him with it. Since
then no one addressed a word to Tatiana.
And all this cost him nothing. It is true
the wardrobe-maid, as soon as she reached
the maids' room, promptly fell into a faint-
ing-fit, and behaved altogether so skilfully
that Gerasim's rough action reached his mistress's knowledge the same day. But the

capricious old lady only laughed, and several times, to the great offence of the wardrobe-maid, forced her to repeat "how he bent your head down with his heavy hand," and next day she sent Gerasim a rouble. She looked on him with favour as a strong and faithful watchman. Gerasim stood in considerable awe of her, but, all the same, he had hopes of her favour, and was preparing to go to her with a petition for leave to marry Tatiana. He was only waiting for a new coat, promised him by the steward, to present a proper appearance before his mistress, when this same mistress suddenly took it into her head to marry Tatiana to Kapiton.

The reader will now readily understand the perturbation of mind that overtook the steward Gavrila after his conversation with his mistress. "My lady," he thought, as he sat at the window, "favours Gerasim, to be sure"—(Gavrila was well aware of this, and that was why he himself looked on him with an indulgent eye)—"still he is a speechless creature. I could not, indeed, put it before the mistress that Gerasim's courting Tatiana. But, after all, it's true enough; he's a queer sort of husband. But on the other hand, that

devil, God forgive me, has only got to find
out they're marrying Tatiana to Kapiton,
he'll smash up everything in the house, 'pon
my soul! There's no reasoning with him;
why, he's such a devil, God forgive my sins,
there's no getting over him no how . . . 'pon
my soul!"

Kapiton's entrance broke the thread of
Gavrila's reflections. The dissipated shoemaker came in, his hands behind him, and
lounging carelessly against a projecting an-
gle of the wall, near the door, crossed his
right foot in front of his left, and tossed his
head, as much as to say, "What do you
want?"

Gavrila looked at Kapiton, and drummed
with his fingers on the window-frame. Kapiton merely screwed up his leaden eyes a little, but he did not look down, he even grinned
slightly, and passed his hand over his whit-
ish locks which were sticking up in all directions. "Well, here I am. What is it?"

"You're a pretty fellow," said Gavrila, and
paused. "A pretty fellow you are, there's
no denying!"

Kapiton only twitched his little shoulders.
"Are you any better, pray?" he thought to
himself.

"Just look at yourself, now, look at yourself," Gavrila went on reproachfully; "now, what ever do you look like?"

Kapiton serenely surveyed his shabby tattered coat, and his patched trousers, and with special attention stared at his burst boots, especially the one on the tip-toe of which his right foot so gracefully poised, and he fixed his eyes again on the steward.

"Well?"

"Well?" repeated Gavrila. "Well? And then you say well? You look like old Nick himself, God forgive my saying so, that's what you look like."

Kapiton blinked rapidly.

"Go on abusing me, go on, if you like, Gavrila Andreitch," he thought to himself again.

"Here you've been drunk again," Gavrila began, "drunk again, haven't you? Eh? Come, answer me!"

"Owing to the weakness of my health, I have exposed myself to spirituous beverages, certainly," replied Kapiton.

"Owing to the weakness of your health! ... They let you off too easy, that's what it is; and you've been apprenticed in Petersburg.... Much you learned in your apprenticeship! You simply eat your bread in idleness."

"In that matter, Gavrila Andreitch, there is one to judge me, the Lord God Himself, and no one else. He also knows what manner of man I be in this world, and whether I eat my bread in idleness. And as concerning your contention regarding drunkenness, in that matter, too, I am not to blame, but rather a friend; he led me into temptation, but was diplomatic and got away, while I . . ."

"While you were left, like a goose, in the street. Ah, you're a dissolute fellow! But that's not the point," the steward went on, "I've something to tell you. Our lady . . ." here he paused a minute, "it's our lady's pleasure that you should be married. Do you hear? She imagines you may be steadier when you're married. Do you understand?"

"To be sure I do."

"Well, then. For my part I think it would be better to give you a good hiding. But there—it's her business. Well? are you agreeable?"

Kapiton grinned.

"Matrimony is an excellent thing for any

one, Gavrila Andreitch; and, as far as I am concerned, I shall be quite agreeable."

"Very well, then," replied Gavrila, while he reflected to himself: "there's no denying the man expresses himself very properly. Only there's one thing," he pursued aloud: "the wife our lady's picked out for you is an unlucky choice."

"Why, who is she, permit me to inquire?"

"Tatiana."

"Tatiana?"

And Kapiton opened his eyes, and moved a little away from the wall.

"Well, what are you in such a taking for? . . . Isn't she to your taste, hey?"

"Not to my taste, do you say, Gavrila Andreitch? She's right enough, a hard-working steady girl. . . . But you know very well yourself, Gavrila Andreitch, why that fellow, that wild man of the woods, that monster of the steppes, he's after her, you know. . . ."

"I know, mate, I know all about it," the butler cut him short in a tone of annoyance: "but there, you see . . ."

"But upon my soul, Gavrila Andreitch! why, he'll kill me, by God, he will, he'll crush me like some fly; why, he's got a fist—why,

you kindly look yourself what a fist he's got;
why, he's simply got a fist like Minin Pozhar-
sky's. You see he's deaf, he beats and does
not hear how he's beating! He swings his
great fists, as if he's asleep. And there's no
possibility of pacifying him; and for why?
Why, because, as you know yourself, Gavrila
Andreitch, he's deaf, and what's more, has
no more wit than the heel of my foot. Why,
he's a sort of beast, a heathen idol, Gavrila
Andreitch, and worse . . . a block of wood;
what have I done that I should have to suffer
from him now? Sure it is, it's all over with
me now; I've knocked about, I've had enough
to put up with, I've been battered like an
earthenware pot, but still I'm a man, after
all, and not a worthless pot."

"I know, I know, don't go talking
away. . . ."

"Lord, my God!" the shoemaker continued
warmly, "when is the end? when, O Lord!
A poor wretch I am, a poor wretch whose
sufferings are endless! What a life, what a
life mine's been, come to think of it! In
my young days, I was beaten by a German
I was 'prentice to; in the prime of life beat-
en by my own countrymen, and last of all,

in ripe years, see what I have been brought
to. . . ."

"Ugh, you flabby soul!" said Gavrila
Andreitch. "Why do you make so many
words about it?"

"Why, do you say, Gavrila Andreitch? It's
not a beating I'm afraid of, Gavrila Andreitch. A gentleman may chastise me in
private, but give me a civil word before folks,
and I'm a man still; but see now, whom I've
to do with. . . ."

"Come, get along," Gavrila interposed im-
patiently. Kapiton turned away and staggered off.

"But, if it were not for him," the steward
shouted after him, "you would consent for
your part?"

"I signify my acquiescence," retorted Kapiton as he disappeared.

His fine language did not desert him, even
in the most trying positions.

The steward walked several times up and
down the room.

"Well, call Tatiana now," he said at last.

A few instants later, Tatiana had come up
almost noiselessly, and was standing in the
doorway.

"What are your orders, Gavrila Andreitch?" she said in a soft voice.

The steward looked at her intently.

"Well, Taniusha," he said, "would you like to be married? Our lady has chosen a husband for you."

"Yes, Gavrila Andreitch. And whom has she deigned to name as a husband for me?" she added falteringly.

"Kapiton, the shoemaker."

"Yes, sir."

"He's a feather-brained fellow, that's certain. But it's just for that the mistress reckons upon you."

"Yes, sir."

"There's one difficulty . . . you know the deaf man, Gerasim, he's courting you, you see. How did you come to bewitch such a bear? But you see, he'll kill you, very like, he's such a bear. . . ."

"He'll kill me, Gavrila Andreitch, he'll kill me, and no mistake."

"Kill you. . . . Well, we shall see about that. What do you mean by saying he'll kill you? Has he any right to kill you? tell me yourself."

"I don't know, Gavrila Andreitch, about his having any right or not."

"What a woman! why, you've made him no promise, I suppose. . . ."

"What are you pleased to ask of me?"

The steward was silent for a little, thinking, "You're a meek soul! Well, that's right," he said aloud; "we'll have another talk with you later, now you can go, Taniusha; I see you're not unruly, certainly."

Tatiana turned, steadied herself a little against the doorpost, and went away.

"And, perhaps, our lady will forget all about this wedding by to-morrow," thought the steward; "and here am I worrying myself for nothing! As for that insolent fellow, we must tie him down, if it comes to that, we must let the police know. . . ." "Ustinya Fyedorovna!" he shouted in a loud voice to his wife, "heat the samovar, my good soul. . . ." All that day Tatiana hardly went out of the laundry. At first she had started crying, then she wiped away her tears, and set to work as before. Kapiton stayed till late at night at the ginshop with a friend of his, a man of gloomy appearance, to whom he related in detail how he used to live in Petersburg with a gentleman, who would have been all right, except he was a bit too strict, and he had a slight weakness besides,

he was too fond of drink; and, as to the fair
sex, he didn't stick at anything. His gloomy
companion merely said yes; but when Kapiton announced at last that, in a certain
event, he would have to lay hands on himself
to-morrow, his gloomy companion remarked
that it was bedtime. And they parted in
surly silence.

Meanwhile, the steward's anticipations
were not fulfilled. The old lady was so much
taken up with the idea of Kapiton's wedding,
that even in the night she talked of nothing
else to one of her companions, who was kept
in her house solely to entertain her in case of
sleeplessness, and, like a night cabman, slept
in the day. When Gavrila came to her after
morning tea with his report, her first question was: "And how about our wedding—is
it getting on all right?" He replied, of
course, that it was getting on first rate, and
that Kapiton would appear before her to
pay his reverence to her that day. The old
lady was not quite well; she did not give
much time to business. The steward went
back to his own room, and called a council.
The matter certainly called for serious consideration. Tatiana would make no difficulty, of course; but Kapiton had declared

in the hearing of all that he had but one
head to lose, not two or three. . . . Gerasim
turned rapid sullen looks on every one, would
not budge from the steps of the maids' quar-
ters, and seemed to guess that some mischief
was being hatched against him. They met
together. Among them was an old sideboard
waiter, nicknamed Uncle Tail, to whom every
one looked respectfully for counsel, though
all they got out of him was, "Here's a pretty
pass! to be sure, to be sure, to be sure!"
As a preliminary measure of security, to pro-
vide against contingencies, they locked Kapiton up in the lumber-room where the filter
was kept; then considered the question with
the gravest deliberation. It would, to be
sure, be easy to have recourse to force. But
Heaven save us! there would be an uproar,
the mistress would be put out—it would be
awful! What should they do? They thought
and thought, and at last thought out a solu-
tion. It had many a time been observed
that Gerasim could not bear drunkards . . .
As he sat at the gates, he would always turn
away with disgust when some one passed by
intoxicated, with unsteady steps and his cap
on one side of his ear. They resolved that
Tatiana should be instructed to pretend to

be tipsy, and should pass by Gerasim stag-
gering and reeling about. The poor girl re-
fused for a long while to agree to this, but
they persuaded her at last; she saw, too, that
it was the only possible way of getting rid
of her adorer. She went out. Kapiton was
released from the lumber-room; for, after
all, he had an interest in the affair. Gerasim
was sitting on the curb-stone at the gates
scraping the ground with a spade. . . . From
behind every corner, from behind every win-
dow-blind, the others were watching him. . . .
The trick succeeded beyond all expectations.
On seeing Tatiana, at first, he nodded as
usual, making caressing, inarticulate sounds;
then he looked carefully at her, dropped his
spade, jumped up, went up to her, brought
his face close to her face. . . . In her fright
she staggered more than ever, and shut her
eyes. . . . He took her by the arm, whirled
her right across the yard, and going into the
room where the council had been sitting,
pushed her straight at Kapiton. Tatiana
fairly swooned away. . . . Gerasim stood,
looked at her, waved his hand, laughed, and
went off, stepping heavily, to his garret. . . .
For the next twenty-four hours, he did not
come out of it. The postillion Antipka said

afterwards that he saw Gerasim through a crack in the wall, sitting on his bedstead, his face in his hand. From time to time he uttered soft regular sounds; he was wailing a dirge, that is, swaying backwards and forwards with his eyes shut, and shaking his head as drivers or bargemen do when they chant their melancholy songs. Antipka could not bear it, and he came away from the crack. When Gerasim came out of the garret next day, no particular change could be observed in him. He only seemed, as it were, more morose, and took not the slightest notice of Tatiana or Kapiton. The same evening, they both had to appear before their mistress with geese under their arms, and in a week's time they were married. Even on the day of the wedding Gerasim showed no change of any sort in his behaviour. Only, he came back from the river without water, he had somehow broken the barrel on the road; and at night, in the stable, he washed and rubbed down his horse so vigorously, that it swayed like a blade of grass in the wind, and staggered from one leg to the other under his fists of iron.

All this had taken place in the spring. Another year passed by, during which Kapi-

ton became a hopeless drunkard, and as being absolutely of no use for anything, was
sent away with the store waggons to a dis-
tant village with his wife. On the day of his
departure, he put a very good face on it at
first, and declared that he would always be
at home, send him where they would, even
to the other end of the world; but later on
he lost heart, began grumbling that he was
being taken to uneducated people, and col-
lapsed so completely at last that he could
not even put his own hat on. Some charita-
ble soul stuck it on his forehead, set the
peak straight in front, and thrust it on with
a slap from above. When everything was
quite ready, and the peasants already held
the reins in their hands, and were only waiting for the words "With God's blessing!" to
start, Gerasim came out of his garret, went
up to Tatiana, and gave her as a parting
present a red cotton handkerchief he had
bought for her a year ago. Tatiana, who
had up to that instant borne all the revolt-
ing details of her life with great indifference, could not control herself upon that;
she burst into tears, and as she took her seat
in the cart, she kissed Gerasim three times
like a good Christian. He meant to accom-

pany her as far as the town-barrier, and did walk beside her cart for a while, but he stopped suddenly at the Crimean ford, waved his hand, and walked away along the river-side. .

It was getting towards evening. He walked slowly, watching the water. All of a sudden he fancied something was floundering in the mud close to the bank. He stooped over, and saw a little white-and-black puppy, who, in spite of all its efforts, could not get out of the water; it was struggling, slipping back, and trembling all over its thin wet little body. Gerasim looked at the unlucky little dog, picked it up with one hand, put it into the bosom of his coat, and hurried with long steps homewards. He went into his garret, put the rescued puppy on his bed, covered it with his thick overcoat, ran first to the stable for straw, and then to the kitchen for a cup of milk. Carefully folding back the overcoat, and spreading out the straw, he set the milk on the bedstead. The poor little puppy was not more than three weeks old, its eyes were only just open—one eye still seemed rather larger than the other; it did not know how to lap out of a cup, and did nothing but shiver and blink. Gerasim took hold of its head

softly with two fingers, and dipped its little
nose into the milk. The pup suddenly began
lapping greedily, sniffing, shaking itself, and
choking. Gerasim watched and watched it,
and all at once he laughed outright. . . . All
night long he was waiting on it, keeping it
covered, and rubbing it dry. He fell asleep
himself at last, and slept quietly and happily
by its side.

No mother could have looked after her
baby as Gerasim looked after his little nurs-
ling. At first, she—for the pup turned out
to be a bitch—was very weak, feeble, and
ugly, but by degrees she grew stronger and
improved in looks, and thanks to the unflag-
ging care of her preserver, in eight months'
time she was transformed into a very pretty
dog of the spaniel breed, with long ears, a
bushy spiral tail, and large expressive eyes.
She was devotedly attached to Gerasim, and
was never a yard from his side; she always
followed him about wagging her tail. He
had even given her a name—the dumb know
that their inarticulate noises call the attention of others. He called her Mumu. All
the servants in the house liked her, and called
her Mumu, too. She was very intelligent,
she was friendly with every one, but was only

fond of Gerasim. Gerasim, on his side, loved
her passionately, and he did not like it when
other people stroked her; whether he was
afraid for her, or jealous—God knows! She
used to wake him in the morning, pulling at
his coat; she used to take the reins in her
mouth, and bring him up the old horse that
carried the water, with whom she was on very
friendly terms. With a face of great impor-
tance, she used to go with him to the river;
she used to watch his brooms and spades, and
never allowed any one to go into his garret.
He cut a little hole in his door on purpose
for her, and she seemed to feel that only in
Gerasim's garret she was completely mistress
and at home; and directly she went in, she
used to jump with a satisfied air upon the
bed. At night she did not sleep at all, but
she never barked without sufficient cause,
like some stupid house-dog, who, sitting on
its hind-legs, blinking, with its nose in the
air, barks simply from dulness, at the stars,
usually three times in succession. No!
Mumu's delicate little voice was never raised
without good reason; either some stranger
was passing close to the fence, or there was
some suspicious sound or rustle somewhere.
... In fact, she was an excellent watch-dog.

It is true that there was another dog in the
yard, a tawny old dog with brown spots,
called Wolf, but he was never, even at night,
let off the chain; and, indeed, he was so
decrepit that he did not even wish for freedom. He used to lie curled up in his ken-
nel, and only rarely uttered a sleepy, almost
noiseless bark, which broke off at once, as
though he were himself aware of its useless-
ness. Mumu never went into the mistress's
house; and when Gerasim carried wood into
the rooms, she always stayed behind, impa-
tiently waiting for him at the steps, pricking
up her ears and turning her head to right
and to left at the slightest creak of the
door. . . .

So passed another year. Gerasim went on
performing his duties as house-porter, and
was very well content with his lot, when
suddenly an unexpected incident occurred.
. . . One fine summer day the old lady was
walking up and down the drawing-room with
her dependants. She was in high spirits; she
laughed and made jokes. Her servile companions laughed and joked too, but they did
not feel particularly mirthful; the household
did not much like it, when their mistress was
in a lively mood, for, to begin with, she ex-

pected from every one prompt and complete participation in her merriment, and was furious if any one showed a face that did not beam with delight, and secondly, these outbursts never lasted long with her, and were usually followed by a sour and gloomy mood. That day she had got up in a lucky hour; at cards she took the four knaves, which means the fulfilment of one's wishes (she used to try her fortune on the cards every morning), and her tea struck her as particularly delicious, for which her maid was rewarded by words of praise, and by twopence in money. With a sweet smile on her wrinkled lips, the lady walked about the drawing-room and went up to the window. A flower-garden had been laid out before the window, and in the very middle bed, under a rose-bush, lay Mumu busily gnawing a bone. The lady caught sight of her.

"Mercy on us!" she cried suddenly; "what dog is that?"

The companion, addressed by the old lady, hesitated, poor thing, in that wretched state of uneasiness which is common in any person in a dependent position who doesn't know very well what significance to give to the exclamation of a superior.

"I d . . . d . . . don't know," she faltered:
"I fancy it's the dumb man's dog."

"Mercy!" the lady cut her short: "but it's
a charming little dog! order it to be brought
in. Has he had it long? How is it I've never
seen it before? . . . Order it to be brought
in."

The companion flew at once into the hall.

"Boy, boy!" she shouted: "bring Mumu in
at once! She's in the flower-garden."

"Her name's Mumu then," observed the
lady: "a very nice name."

"Oh, very, indeed!" chimed in the companion. "Make haste, Stepan!"

Stepan, a sturdily-built young fellow,
whose duties were those of a footman, rushed
headlong into the flower-garden, and tried
to capture Mumu, but she cleverly slipped
from his fingers, and with her tail in the air,
fled full speed to Gerasim, who was at that
instant in the kitchen, knocking out and
cleaning a barrel, turning it upside down in
his hands like a child's drum. Stepan ran
after her, and tried to catch her just at
her master's feet; but the sensible dog would
not let a stranger touch her, and with a
bound, she got away. Gerasim looked on with
a smile at all this ado; at last, Stepan got

up, much amazed, and hurriedly explained to him by signs that the mistress wanted the dog brought in to her. Gerasim was a little astonished; he called Mumu, however, picked her up, and handed her over to Stepan. Stepan carried her into the drawing-room, and put her down on the parquette floor. The old lady began calling the dog to her in a coaxing voice. Mumu, who had never in her life been in such magnificent apartments, was very much frightened, and made a rush for the door, but, being driven back by the obsequious Stepan, she began trembling, and huddled close up against the wall.

"Mumu, Mumu, come to me, come to your mistress," said the lady; "come, silly thing . . . don't be afraid."

"Come, Mumu, come to the mistress," repeated the companions. "Come along!"

But Mumu looked round her uneasily, and did not stir.

"Bring her something to eat," said the old lady. "How stupid she is! she won't come to her mistress. What's she afraid of?"

"She's not used to your honour yet," ventured one of the companions in a timid and conciliatory voice.

Stepan brought in a saucer of milk, and

set it down before Mumu, but Mumu would
not even sniff at the milk, and still shivered,
and looked round as before.

"Ah, what a silly you are!" said the lady,
and going up to her, she stooped down, and
was about to stroke her, but Mumu turned
her head abruptly, and showed her teeth.
The lady hurriedly drew back her hand. . . .

A momentary silence followed. Mumu gave
a faint whine, as though she would complain
and apologise. . . . The old lady moved back,
scowling. The dog's sudden movement had
frightened her.

"Ah!" shrieked all the companions at once,
"she's not bitten you, has she? Heaven forbid! (Mumu had never bitten any one in her
life.) Ah! ah!"

"Take her away," said the old lady in a
changed voice. "Wretched little dog! What
a spiteful creature!"

And, turning round deliberately, she went
towards her boudoir. Her companions looked
timidly at one another, and were about to
follow her, but she stopped, stared coldly at
them, and said, "What's that for, pray? I've
not called you," and went out.

The companions waved their hands to
Stepan in despair. He picked up Mumu,

and flung her promptly outside the door, just
at Gerasim's feet, and half-an-hour later a
profound stillness reigned in the house, and
the old lady sat on her sofa looking blacker
than a thundercloud.

What trifles, if you think of it, will sometimes disturb any one!

Till evening the lady was out of humour;
she did not talk to any one, did not play
cards, and passed a bad night. She fancied
the eau-de-Cologne they gave her was not
the same as she usually had, and that her pil-
low smelt of soap, and she made the wardrobe-maid smell all the bed linen—in fact she
was very upset and cross altogether. Next
morning she ordered Gavrila to be summoned
an hour earlier than usual.

"Tell me, please," she began, directly the
latter, not without some inward trepidation,
crossed the threshold of her boudoir, "what
dog was that barking all night in our yard?
It wouldn't let me sleep!"

"A dog, 'm . . . what dog, 'm . . . may be,
the dumb man's dog, 'm," he brought out in
a rather unsteady voice.

"I don't know whether it was the dumb
man's or whose, but it wouldn't let me sleep.
And I wonder what we have such a lot of

dogs for! I wish to know. We have a yard dog, haven't we?"

"Oh, yes, 'm, we have, 'm. Wolf, 'm."

"Well, why more, what do we want more dogs for? It's simply introducing disorder. There's no one in control in the house—that's what it is. And what does the dumb man want with a dog? Who gave him leave to keep dogs in my yard? Yesterday I went to the window, and there it was lying in the flower-garden; it had dragged in some nastiness it was gnawing, and my roses are planted there. . . ."

The lady ceased.

"Let her be gone from to-day . . . do you hear?"

"Yes, 'm."

"To-day. Now go. I will send for you later for the report."

Gavrila went away.

As he went through the drawing-room, the steward by way of maintaining order moved a bell from one table to another; he stealthily blew his duck-like nose in the hall, and went into the outer-hall. In the outer-hall, on a locker was Stepan asleep in the attitude of a slain warrior in a battalion picture, his bare legs thrust out below the coat which served

him for a blanket. The steward gave him a
shove, and whispered some instructions to
him, to which Stepan responded with something between a yawn and a laugh. The
steward went away, and Stepan got up, put
on his coat and his boots, went out and stood
on the steps. Five minutes had not passed
before Gerasim made his appearance with a
huge bundle of hewn logs on his back, ac-
companied by the inseparable Mumu. (The
lady had given orders that her bedroom and
boudoir should be heated at times even in
the summer.) Gerasim turned sideways before the door, shoved it open with his shoulder, and staggered into the house with his
load. Mumu, as usual, stayed behind to wait
for him. Then Stepan, seizing his chance,
suddenly pounced on her, like a kite on a
chicken, held her down to the ground, gathered her up in his arms, and without even
putting on his cap, ran out of the yard with
her, got into the first fly he met, and gal-
loped off to a market-place. There he soon
found a purchaser, to whom he sold her for
a shilling, on condition that he would keep
her for at least a week tied up; then he returned at once. But before he got home, he
got off the fly, and going right round the

yard, jumped over the fence into the yard
from a back street. He was afraid to go in
at the gate for fear of meeting Gerasim.

His anxiety was unnecessary, however;
Gerasim was no longer in the yard. On
coming out of the house he had at once
missed Mumu. He never remembered her
failing to wait for his return, and began running up and down, looking for her, and calling her in his own way. . . . He rushed up
to his garret, up to the hay-loft, ran out into
the street, this way and that. . . . She was
lost! He turned to the other serfs, with the
most despairing signs, questioned them about
her, pointing to her height from the ground,
describing her with his hands. . . . Some of
them really did not know what had become of
Mumu, and merely shook their heads, others
did know, and smiled to him for all response,
while the steward assumed an important air,
and began scolding the coachman. Then
Gerasim ran right away out of the yard.

It was dark by the time he came back.
From his worn-out look, his unsteady walk,
and his dusty clothes, it might be surmised
that he had been running over half Moscow.
He stood still opposite the windows of the
mistress's house, took a searching look at the

steps where a group of house-serfs were crowded together, turned away, and uttered once more his inarticulate "Mumu." Mumu did not answer. He went away. Every one looked after him, but no one smiled or said a word, and the inquisitive postillion Antipka reported next morning in the kitchen that the dumb man had been groaning all night.

All the next day Gerasim did not show himself, so that they were obliged to send the coachman Potap for water instead of him, at which the coachman Potap was anything but pleased. The lady asked Gavrila if her orders had been carried out. Gavrila replied that they had. The next morning Gerasim came out of his garret, and went about his work. He came in to his dinner, ate it, and went out again, without a greeting to any one. His face, which had always been lifeless, as with all deaf-mutes, seemed now to be turned to stone. After dinner he went out of the yard again, but not for long; he came back, and went straight up to the hayloft. Night came on, a clear moonlight night. Gerasim lay breathing heavily, and incessantly turning from side to side. Suddenly he felt something pull at the skirt of his coat. He started, but did not raise his head, and even shut his eyes tighter. But again there was a pull, stronger than before; he jumped up . . . before him, with an end of string round her neck, was Mumu, twisting and turning. A prolonged cry of delight broke from his speechless breast; he caught up Mumu, and hugged her tight in his arms, she licked his nose and eyes, and beard and moustache, all in one instant. . . . He stood a little, thought a minute, crept cautiously down from the hay-loft, looked round, and having satisfied himself that no one could see him, made his way successfully to his garret. Gerasim had guessed before that his dog had not got lost by her own doing, that she must have been taken away by the mistress's orders; the servants had explained to him by signs that his Mumu had snapped at her, and he determined to take his own measures. First he fed Mumu with a bit of bread, fondled her, and put her to bed, then he fell to meditating, and spent the whole night long in meditating how he could best conceal her. At last he decided to leave her all day in the garret, and only to come in now and then to see her, and to take her out at night. The hole in the door he stopped up effectually with his old overcoat, and almost

before it was light he was already in the
yard, as though nothing had happened, even
—innocent guile!—the same expression of
melancholy on his face. It did not even oc-
cur to the poor deaf man that Mumu would
betray herself by her whining; in reality,
every one in the house was soon aware that
the dumb man's dog had come back, and was
locked up in his garret, but from sympathy
with him and with her, and partly, perhaps,
from dread of him, they did not let him know
that they had found out his secret. The
steward scratched his head, and gave a despairing wave of his hand, as much as to say,
"Well, well, God have mercy on him! If
only it doesn't come to the mistress's ears!"
But the dumb man had never shown such
energy as on that day; he cleaned and scraped
the whole courtyard, pulled up every single
weed with his own hand, tugged up every
stake in the fence of the flower-garden, to
satisfy himself that they were strong enough,
and unaided drove them in again; in fact, he
toiled and laboured so that even the old lady
noticed his zeal. Twice in the course of the
day Gerasim went stealthily in to see his
prisoner; when night came on, he lay down
to sleep with her in the garret, not in the

hay-loft, and only at two o'clock in the night
he went out to take her a turn in the fresh
air. After walking about the courtyard a
good while with her, he was just turning
back, when suddenly a rustle was heard behind the fence on the side of the back street.
Mumu pricked up her ears, growled—went up
to the fence, sniffed, and gave vent to a loud
shrill bark. Some drunkard had thought fit
to take refuge under the fence for the night.
At that very time the old lady had just
fallen asleep after a prolonged fit of "nervous
agitation"; these fits of agitation always overtook her after too hearty a supper. The sudden bark waked her up: her heart palpitated,
and she felt faint. "Girls, girls!" she
moaned. "Girls!" The terrified maids ran
into her bedroom. "Oh, oh, I am dying!"
she said, flinging her arms about in her agitation. "Again, that dog again! . . . Oh, send
for the doctor. They mean to be the death
of me. . . . The dog, the dog again! Oh!"
And she let her head fall back, which always
signified a swoon. They rushed for the doctor, that is, for the household physician, Har-
iton. This doctor, whose whole qualification
consisted in wearing soft-soled boots, knew
how to feel the pulse delicately. He used to

sleep fourteen hours out of the twenty-four,
but the rest of the time he was always sigh-
ing, and continually dosing the old lady with
cherrybay drops. This doctor ran up at once,
fumigated the room with burnt feathers, and
when the old lady opened her eyes, promptly
offered her a wineglass of the hallowed drops
on a silver tray. The old lady took them,
but began again at once in a tearful voice
complaining of the dog, of Gavrila, and of
her fate, declaring that she was a poor old
woman, and that every one had forsaken her,
no one pitied her, every one wished her dead.
Meanwhile the luckless Mumu had gone on
barking, while Gerasim tried in vain to call
her away from the fence. "There . . . there
. . . again," groaned the old lady, and once
more she turned up the whites of her eyes.
The doctor whispered to a maid, she rushed
into the outer-hall, and shook Stepan, he ran
to wake Gavrila, Gavrila in a fury ordered
the whole household to get up.

Gerasim turned round, saw lights and shadows moving in the windows, and with an in-
stinct of coming trouble in his heart, put
Mumu under his arm, ran into his garret, and
locked himself in. A few minutes later five
men were banging at his door, but feeling

the resistance of the bolt, they stopped.
Gavrila ran up in a fearful state of mind, and
ordered them all to wait there and watch till
morning. Then he flew off himself to the
maids' quarter, and through an old companion, Liubov Liubimovna, with whose as-
sistance he used to steal tea, sugar, and
other groceries and to falsify the accounts,
sent word to the mistress that the dog had
unhappily run back from somewhere, but
that to-morrow she should be killed, and
would the mistress be so gracious as not to
be angry and to overlook it. The old lady
would probably not have been so soon ap-
peased, but the doctor had in his haste given
her fully forty drops instead of twelve. The
strong dose of narcotic acted; in a quarter
of an hour the old lady was in a sound and
peaceful sleep; while Gerasim was lying with
a white face on his bed, holding Mumu's
mouth tightly shut.

Next morning the lady woke up rather late.
Gavrila was waiting till she should be awake,
to give the order for a final assault on
Gerasim's stronghold, while he prepared himself to face a fearful storm. But the storm
did not come off. The old lady lay in bed

and sent for the eldest of her dependent
companions.

"Liubov Liubimovna," she began in a sub-
dued weak voice—she was fond of playing
the part of an oppressed and forsaken vic-
tim; needless to say, every one in the house
was made extremely uncomfortable at such
times—"Liubov Liubimovna, you see my position; go, my love, to Gavrila Andreitch, and
talk to him a little. Can he really prize some
wretched cur above the repose—the very life
—of his mistress? I could not bear to think
so," she added, with an expression of deep
feeling. "Go, my love; be so good as to go
to Gavrila Andreitch for me."

Liubov Liubimovna went to Gavrila's room.
What conversation passed between them is
not known, but a short time after, a whole
crowd of people was moving across the yard
in the direction of Gerasim's garret. Gavrila
walked in front, holding his cap on with his
hand, though there was no wind. The foot-
men and cooks were close behind him; Uncle
Tail was looking out of a window, giving instructions, that is to say, simply waving his
hands. At the rear there was a crowd of
small boys skipping and hopping along; half
of them were outsiders who had run up. On

the narrow staircase leading to the garret
sat one guard; at the door were standing two
more with sticks. They began to mount the
stairs, which they entirely blocked up. Gavrila went up to the door, knocked with his
fist, shouting, "Open the door!"

A stifled bark was audible, but there was
no answer.

"Open the door, I tell you," he repeated.

"But, Gavrila Andreitch," Stepan observed
from below, "he's deaf, you know—he doesn't
hear."

They all laughed.

"What are we to do?" Gavrila rejoined
from above.

"Why, there's a hole there in the door,"
answered Stepan, "so you shake the stick in
there."

Gavrila bent down.

"He's stuffed it up with a coat or something."

"Well, you just push the coat in."

At this moment a smothered bark was
heard again.

"See, see—she speaks for herself," was remarked in the crowd, and again they laughed.

Gavrila scratched his ear.

"No, mate," he responded at last, "you can poke the coat in yourself, if you like."

"All right, let me."

And Stepan scrambled up, took the stick, pushed in the coat, and began waving the stick about in the opening, saying, "Come out, come out!" as he did so. He was still waving the stick, when suddenly the door of the garret was flung open; all the crowd flew pell-mell down the stairs instantly, Gavrila first of all. Uncle Tail locked the window.

"Come, come, come," shouted Gavrila from the yard, "mind what you're about."

Gerasim stood without stirring in his doorway. The crowd gathered at the foot of the stairs. Gerasim, with his arms akimbo, looked down at all these poor creatures in German coats; in his red peasant's shirt he looked like a giant before them. Gavrila took a step forward.

"Mind, mate," said he, "don't be insolent."

And he began to explain to him by signs that the mistress insists on having his dog; that he must hand it over at once, or it would be the worse for him.

Gerasim looked at him, pointed to the dog, made a motion with his hand round his neck, as though he were pulling a noose tight, and glanced with a face of inquiry at the steward.

"Yes, yes," the latter assented, nodding; "yes, just so."

Gerasim dropped his eyes, then all of a sudden roused himself and pointed to Mumu, who was all the while standing beside him, innocently wagging her tail and pricking up her ears inquisitively. Then he repeated the strangling action round his neck and significantly struck himself on the breast, as though announcing he would take upon himself the task of killing Mumu.

"But you'll deceive us," Gavrila waved back in response.

Gerasim looked at him, smiled scornfully, struck himself again on the breast, and slammed-to the door.

They all looked at one another in silence.

"What does that mean?" Gavrila began. "He's locked himself in."

"Let him be, Gavrila Andreitch," Stepan advised, "he'll do it if he's promised. He's like that, you know. . . . If he makes a promise, it's a certain thing. He's not like us others in that. The truth's the truth with him. Yes, indeed."

"Yes," they all repeated, nodding their heads, "yes—that's so—yes."

Uncle Tail opened his window, and he too
said, "Yes."

"Well, may be, we shall see," responded
Gavrila; "any way, we won't take off the
guard. Here you, Eroshka!" he added, addressing a poor fellow in a yellow nankeen
coat, who considered himself to be a gar-
dener, "what have you to do? Take a stick
and sit here, and if anything happens, run
to me at once!"

Eroshka took a stick, and sat down on the
bottom stair. The crowd dispersed, all except a few inquisitive small boys, while Gavrila went home and sent word through Liubov Liubimovna to the mistress, that everything had been done, while he sent a postillion
for a policeman in case of need. The old
lady tied a knot in her handkerchief, sprinkled some eau-de-Cologne on it, sniffed at it,
and rubbed her temples with it, drank some
tea, and, being still under the influence of the
cherrybay drops, fell asleep again.

An hour after all this hubbub the garret
door opened, and Gerasim showed himself.
He had on his best coat; he was leading
Mumu by a string. Eroshka moved aside and
let him pass. Gerasim went to the gates. All
the small boys in the yard stared at him in

silence. He did not even turn round; he only put his cap on in the street. Gavrila sent the same Eroshka to follow him and keep watch on him as a spy. Eroshka, seeing from a distance that he had gone into a cookshop with his dog, waited for him to come out again.

Gerasim was well known at the cookshop, and his signs were understood. He asked for cabbage soup with meat in it, and sat down with his arms on the table. Mumu stood beside his chair, looking calmly at him with her intelligent eyes. Her coat was glossy; one could see she had just been combed down. They brought Gerasim the soup. He crumbled some bread into it, cut the meat up small, and put the plate on the ground. Mumu began eating in her usual refined way, her little muzzle daintily held so as scarcely to touch her food. Gerasim gazed a long while at her; two big tears suddenly rolled from his eyes; one fell on the dog's brow, the other into the soup. He shaded his face with his hand. Mumu ate up half the plateful, and came away from it, licking her lips. Gerasim got up, paid for the soup, and went out, followed by the rather perplexed glances of the waiter. Eroshka, seeing Gerasim, hid

round a corner, and letting him get in front,
followed him again.

Gerasim walked without haste, still holding Mumu by a string. When he got to the
corner of the street, he stood still as though
reflecting, and suddenly set off with rapid
steps to the Crimean Ford. On the way he
went into the yard of a house, where a lodge
was being built, and carried away two bricks
under his arm. At the Crimean Ford, he
turned along the bank, went to a place where
there were two little rowing-boats fastened
to stakes (he had noticed them there before),
and jumped into one of them with Mumu.
A lame old man came out of a shed in the
corner of a kitchen-garden and shouted after
him; but Gerasim only nodded, and began
rowing so vigorously, though against stream,
that in an instant he had darted two hundred
yards away. The old man stood for a while,
scratched his back first with the left and then
with the right hand, and went back hobbling
to the shed.

Gerasim rowed on and on. Moscow was
soon left behind. Meadows stretched each
side of the bank, market gardens, fields, and
copses; peasants' huts began to make their
appearance. There was the fragrance of the

country. He threw down his oars, bent his
head down to Mumu, who was sitting facing
him on a dry cross seat—the bottom of the
boat was full of water—and stayed motionless, his mighty hands clasped upon her back,
while the boat was gradually carried back by
the current towards the town. At last Gerasim drew himself up hurriedly, with a sort
of sick anger in his face, he tied up the bricks
he had taken with string, made a running
noose, put it round Mumu's neck, lifted her
up over the river, and for the last time
looked at her. . . . She watched him confid-
ingly and without any fear, faintly wagging
her tail. He turned away, frowned, and
wrung his hands. . . . Gerasim heard nothing, neither the quick shrill whine of Mumu
as she fell, nor the heavy splash of the water;
for him the noisiest day was soundless and
silent as even the stillest night is not silent
to us. When he opened his eyes again, little
wavelets were hurrying over the river, chas-
ing one another; as before they broke against
the boat's side, and only far away behind
wide circles moved widening to the bank.

Directly Gerasim had vanished from Eroshka's sight, the latter returned home and reported what he had seen.

"Well, then," observed Stepan, "he'll drown her. Now we can feel easy about it. If he once promises a thing. . . ."

No one saw Gerasim during the day. He did not have dinner at home. Evening came on; they were all gathered together to supper, except him.

"What a strange creature that Gerasim is!" piped a fat laundrymaid; "fancy, upsetting himself like that over a dog. . . . Upon my word!"

"But Gerasim has been here," Stepan cried all at once, scraping up his porridge with a spoon.

"How? when?"

"Why, a couple of hours ago. Yes, indeed! I ran against him at the gate; he was going out again from here; he was coming out of the yard. I tried to ask him about his dog, but he wasn't in the best of humours, I could see. Well, he gave me a shove; I suppose he only meant to put me out of his way, as if he'd say, 'Let me go, do!' but he fetched me such a crack on my neck, so seriously, that—oh! oh!" And Stepan, who could not help laughing, shrugged up and rubbed the back of his head. "Yes," he added; "he has got a fist; it's something like a fist, there's no denying that!"

They all laughed at Stepan, and after supper they separated to go to bed.

Meanwhile, at that very time, a gigantic figure with a bag on his shoulders and a stick in his hand, was eagerly and persistently stepping out along the T—— highroad. It was Gerasim. He was hurrying on without looking round; hurrying homewards, to his own village, to his own country. After drowning poor Mumu, he had run back to his garret, hurriedly packed a few things together in an old horsecloth, tied it up in a bundle, tossed it on his shoulder, and so was ready. He had noticed the road carefully when he was brought to Moscow; the village his mistress had taken him from lay only about twenty miles off the highroad. He walked along it with a sort of invincible purpose, a desperate and at the same time joyous determination. He walked, his shoulders thrown back and his chest expanded; his eyes were fixed greedily straight before him. He hastened as though his old mother were waiting for him at home, as though she were calling him to her after long wanderings in strange parts, among strangers. The summer

night, that was just drawing in, was still
and warm; on one side, where the sun had
set, the horizon was still light and faintly
flushed with the last glow of the vanished
day; on the other side a blue-grey twilight
had already risen up. The night was coming
up from that quarter. Quails were in hun-
dreds around; corncrakes were calling to one
another in the thickets. . . . Gerasim could
not hear them; he could not hear the delicate
night-whispering of the trees, by which his
strong legs carried him, but he smelt the familiar scent of the ripening rye, which was
wafted from the dark fields; he felt the wind,
flying to meet him—the wind from home—
beat caressingly upon his face, and play with
his hair and his beard. He saw before him
the whitening road homewards, straight as an
arrow. He saw in the sky stars innumerable,
lighting up his way, and stepped out, strong
and bold as a lion, so that when the rising
sun shed its moist rosy light upon the still
fresh and unwearied traveller, already thirty
miles lay between him and Moscow.

In a couple of days he was at home, in his
little hut, to the great astonishment of the
soldier's wife who had been put in there.
After praying before the holy pictures, he

set off at once to the village elder. The village elder was at first surprised; but the hay-cutting had just begun; Gerasim was a first-rate mower, and they put a scythe into his hand on the spot, and he went to mow in his old way, mowing so that the peasants were fairly astounded as they watched his wide sweeping strokes and the heaps he raked together. . . .

In Moscow the day after Gerasim's flight they missed him. They went to his garret, rummaged about in it, and spoke to Gavrila. He came, looked, shrugged his shoulders, and decided that the dumb man had either run away or had drowned himself with his stupid dog. They gave information to the police, and informed the lady. The old lady was furious, burst into tears, gave orders that he was to be found whatever happened, declared she had never ordered the dog to be destroyed, and, in fact, gave Gavrila such a rating that he could do nothing all day but shake his head and murmur, "Well!" until Uncle Tail checked him at last, sympathetically echoing "We-ell!" At last the news came from the country of Gerasim's being there. The old lady was somewhat pacified; at first she issued a mandate for him to be brought back without delay to Moscow; afterwards, however, she declared that such an ungrateful creature was absolutely of no use to her. Soon after this she died herself; and her heirs had no thought to spare for Gerasim; they let their mother's other servants redeem their freedom on payment of an annual rent.

And Gerasim is living still, a lonely man in his lonely hut; he is strong and healthy as before, and does the work of four men as before, and as before is serious and steady. But his neighbours have observed that ever since his return from Moscow he has quite given up the society of women; he will not even look at them, and does not keep even a single dog. "It's his good luck, though," the peasants reason; "that he can get on without female folk; and as for a dog—what need has he of a dog? you wouldn't get a thief to go into his yard for any money!" Such is the fame of the dumb man's Titanic strength.

THE END